A
gift
from
Carson
Gilchrist

1997

BRAVO, AMELIA BEDELIA!

By **Herman Parish**
Pictures by **Lynn Sweat**

Greenwillow Books, New York

Watercolor paints and a black pen were used for the full-color art.
The text type is Kuenstler.

Text copyright © 1997 by Herman S. Parish III
Illustrations copyright © 1997 by Lynn Sweat
All rights reserved. No part of this book may be reproduced or
utilized in any form or by any means, electronic or mechanical,
including photocopying, recording, or by any information storage
and retrieval system, without permission in writing from the Publisher,
Greenwillow Books, a division of William Morrow & Company, Inc.,
1350 Avenue of the Americas, New York, NY 10019.
Printed in Singapore by Tien Wah Press
First Edition 10 9 8 7 6 5 4 3 2 1

▼▼

Library of Congress Cataloging-in-Publication Data
Parish, Herman.
Bravo, Amelia Bedelia! / by Herman Parish ;
pictures by Lynn Sweat.
p.   cm.
Summary: From the time she is sent to pick up the
guest conductor, Amelia Bedelia's normal confusion
causes quite an uproar at the school concert.
ISBN 0-688-15154-X (trade).   ISBN 0-688-15155-8 (lib. bdg.)
[1. Concerts—Fiction.   2. Humorous stories.]
I. Sweat, Lynn, ill.   II. Title.
PZ7.P2185Br   1997   [E]—dc20
96-9589   CIP   AC

For Rosemary,
my lova
—H. P.

For Jennifer
and Sarah
—L. S.

It was the day of the school concert.

Mrs. Rogers was very upset.

"Where is Amelia Bedelia?

I sent her to the station two hours ago

to pick up our new conductor.

The orchestra is waiting to practice, and . . ."

"Yoo-hoo," said Amelia Bedelia.
"I'm back."

"Where is the conductor?"
said Mrs. Rogers.
"I told you to pick up the conductor."
"I tried my best," said Amelia Bedelia.
"But he was too big for me to pick up."

A large man in a blue uniform
followed Amelia Bedelia into the gym.
"Oh, no!" said Mrs. Rogers.
"This man isn't the conductor!"
"He sure is," said Amelia Bedelia.
"Look at his uniform."

"I did not mean a *train* conductor,"
said Mrs. Rogers.
"I meant a *musical* conductor."
"He is very musical,"
said Amelia Bedelia.
"He whistled all the way over here."

Just then a man
in a nice black suit
jogged into the gym.
"I am sorry I am so late," he said.
"No one met me at the station."
"The *real* conductor," said Mrs. Rogers.
"Thank goodness you are here."

"Look, lady," said the other conductor,
"I like music, but I've got a train to catch."
"Catch a train!" said Amelia Bedelia.
"Be sure to use both hands.
Trains are heavy."

"Never mind," said Mrs. Rogers.
"I will drive him back to the station.
Amelia Bedelia, you help the other
conductor."
"Hurry back," said Amelia Bedelia.
"You do not want to miss the concert."

The conductor said hello to the students.

"Let's practice a few numbers," he said.

He waved his baton to start the music.

"One, two, and *three*!"

Amelia Bedelia kept on counting:

"Four, five, and *six*! Seven, eight, and . . ."

"Stop!" said the conductor.

"Did we practice enough numbers?"
asked Amelia Bedelia.

The children giggled.

"Don't count out loud,"
said the conductor.

"You can tap your toe, if you like."

Amelia Bedelia bent over to reach her toes.

Tap, tap, *tap!* Tap, tap, *tap!*

The children began to laugh.

TAP, TAP, *TAP!*

went the conductor's baton.

"Quiet, please. We have to practice."

He waved his baton.

The orchestra began to play.

Amelia Bedelia was enjoying the music

until a bee flew in.

"Shoo!" said Amelia Bedelia. "Go away!"

She tried to swat that bee.

She waved her arms around.

The conductor stopped the music.
"Miss Bedelia, *I* am the conductor.
Only *I* get to wave my arms around."

"Sorry," said Amelia Bedelia.
"There is a bee, see?"
"A-B-C?" asked the conductor.
"We are practicing music,
   not the alphabet."

The orchestra started up again.

So did that bee.

"Excuse me," said Amelia Bedelia.

"May I borrow your pot lids?"

The boy laughed. "Sure. Here you go."

"Bye-bye, bee," said Amelia Bedelia.

Kee-RRRASH!

The music came to a halt.

"Miss Bedelia," shouted the conductor.

"We were playing a B-flat.
Would you call that B-flat?"

Amelia Bedelia looked at the bee.

"Absolutely," said Amelia Bedelia.

"A bee couldn't get any flatter."

"So you read notes," said the conductor.

"Only if they are addressed to me," said Amelia Bedelia.

"Do you play?" asked the conductor.

"I play every day," said Amelia Bedelia.

"Mr. Rogers says I'm an expert at fiddling."

The conductor handed her a violin.

"An expert fiddler," he said.

"Then you must play by ear."

"If you insist," said Amelia Bedelia.
She rubbed her ear across the strings.
"Ouch! Owie! Help!" cried Amelia
Bedelia.
A girl helped her untangle her hair.

"Expert fiddler indeed,"
said the conductor.
"Next time you should
use a bow."
"I'll use ribbons and barrettes, too,"
said Amelia Bedelia.
The conductor shook his head.
"You should try a different instrument."
"Which one?" asked Amelia Bedelia.

"Try the French horn,"
said the conductor.
"Or maybe another
wind instrument.
Or take up something
in the string section."

The audience began to come into the gym.

It was almost time for the concert.

Amelia Bedelia looked sad.

"Is there something I could play today?"

asked Amelia Bedelia.

"Only this," said the conductor.
"Anyone can play the triangle."
Amelia Bedelia was so excited.
She hit the triangle very hard.

"Play it lower!" said the conductor.

Amelia Bedelia sat down on the floor.

"I give up," said the conductor.
"Just hit the triangle *once* after
    the drum roll and when you hear this."
He signaled to a boy to play the chimes.

DINNNGGG·DONNNGG!

"I'll get it," said Amelia Bedelia.
She ran for the nearest door.

"Come back here,"
 said the conductor.
"Didn't you hear that doorbell?"
 asked Amelia Bedelia.
"No one is at the door,"
 said the conductor.
"When you hear those chimes,
 you come in."

"That's easy," said Amelia Bedelia.
 She opened the door and went out.

"Where are you going?" said the conductor.

"I have to go out before I can come in,"
said Amelia Bedelia.

She shut the door behind her.

"Good riddance!" said the conductor.

"I'll let her out after the concert is over."

Every seat in the gym was filled.

Mrs. Rogers got back just in time.

"Now where has Amelia Bedelia gone?"

said Mrs. Rogers.

She introduced the conductor

to the audience.

He waved his baton

and the concert began.

Amelia Bedelia heard the music start.
"I must listen for when to come in,"
she said to herself.
She looked around the storeroom.
"While I wait, maybe I can find
those instruments he told me about.
Where would I find a string section?"

She picked up a piece of rope.
"This is the only string I see,"
said Amelia Bedelia.
"I'll cut off a section later."

Amelia Bedelia looked some more.
"Ah-ha! Wind instruments.
Should I try a big one or a little one?"
She took the little wind instrument.

"Where would they put a French horn?"
said Amelia Bedelia.
She sat down to think.
"YEOW!" she cried.

She looked where she had sat.
"Lucky me—I found *two* horns.
They may not be French, but they'll do."

"Whoops! There's that doorbell again,"
said Amelia Bedelia. "I'm late!"
She flung open the storeroom door.
"Gangway! I'm coming in!"

The cord from the wind instrument
got tangled in her legs.
"Watch out!" said Amelia Bedelia.
She fell into the big bass drum.

Baaa-BOOOOOM!

The drum began to roll.

It rolled right at the conductor.

"Stop!" he yelled. "I said *STOP!*"

It stopped . . . after it ran into him.

The conductor was very mad.
"You ruined the concert, Amelia Bedelia!
What have you got to say for yourself?"
Amelia Bedelia didn't know what to say.
So she did what he had said to do.
She hit the triangle once.

DING!

All the students began to clap and cheer.

"What a cool concert," said a boy.

"I want to play in the orchestra," said a girl.

"Me, too!" said each and every one.

The conductor pulled Amelia Bedelia
out of the drum.
"Was that a good drum roll?"
asked Amelia Bedelia.
"You played it by ear,"
said the conductor.
"I used my whole body,"
said Amelia Bedelia.
Everyone was
standing up
and clapping.
The conductor
and Amelia Bedelia
took a bow.

"My gracious!" said Mrs. Rogers.

"Are you hurt, Amelia Bedelia?"

"I had fun," said Amelia Bedelia.

"But I'd rather fiddle around at home."

"*That* is music to my ears,"
 said the conductor.

The next day Amelia Bedelia made
a "thank you" note for the conductor.
She forgot to sign it.
But somehow the conductor knew
that it was from Amelia Bedelia.

The Great Snail Race

Adapted by Kim Ostrow
Illustrated by Clint Bond and Andy Clark
Based on the teleplay The Great Snail Race by Paul Tibbitt,
Kent Osborne, and Merriwether Williams

It was a sunny morning in Bikini Bottom. A mailman knocked on Squidward's front door. "Aha!" said Squidward. "I can't believe it's finally here."

The mailman glanced at Squidward's signature. "Thank you, Mister . . . mmmmm . . . Tennis Balls."

"That's Tentacles!" corrected Squidward.

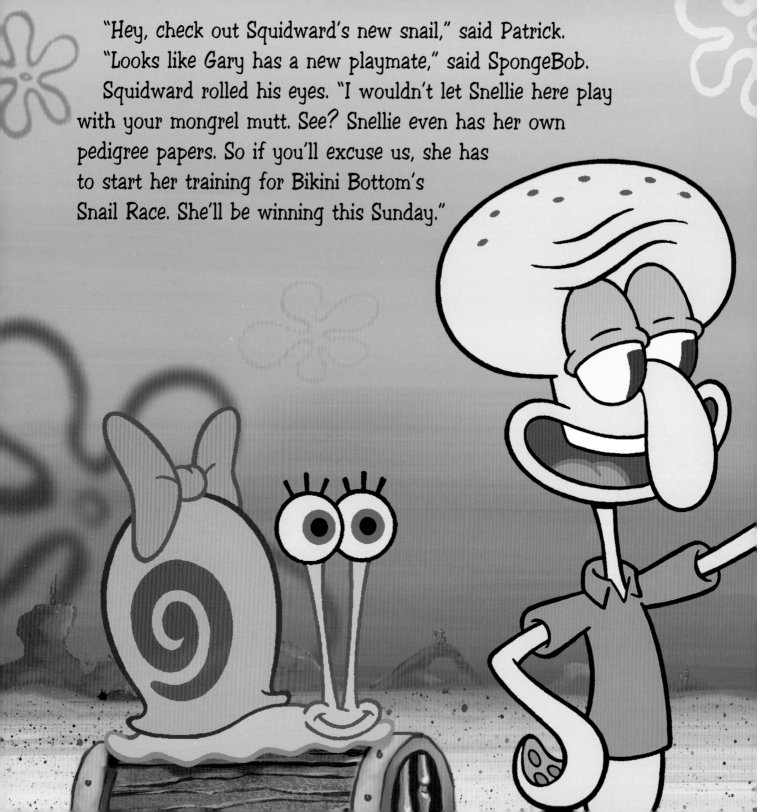

"Hey, check out Squidward's new snail," said Patrick.
"Looks like Gary has a new playmate," said SpongeBob.
Squidward rolled his eyes. "I wouldn't let Snellie here play
with your mongrel mutt. See? Snellie even has her own
pedigree papers. So if you'll excuse us, she has
to start her training for Bikini Bottom's
Snail Race. She'll be winning this Sunday."

"Well, I guess I can't enter Gary in that," said SpongeBob. "Sunday's laundry day!"

Squidward sighed. "You can't enter Gary because Gary isn't a purebred! But Snellie has papers!" he said. He shoved his fancy document toward SpongeBob.

"Hmmm . . . 'Property of Squidward Tentpoles,'" Patrick read.

"That's Tentacles!" corrected Squidward.

CERTIFICATE OF PEDIGREE
Snellie
PROPERTY OF SQUIDWARD TENTACLES

"Patrick, are you thinking what I'm thinking?" asked SpongeBob.

"Yeah," said Patrick. "I should get a snail and enter it in that race and beat Squidward."

"No, no, no!" shouted SpongeBob. "I'm thinking of entering Gary in that race and beating Squidward's snail."

SpongeBob had a lot of work to do to whip Gary into shape. First, he
made a nutritional smoothie for his snail.

"Meow," said Gary.

"Well, of course I expect you to eat this," said SpongeBob. "It's
scientifically designed to help you win tomorrow."

Gary took one look at the drink and slithered out of the room.

Patrick came over to show SpongeBob his new snail.

"Your snail is a rock," said SpongeBob.

"Yeah, I know," said Patrick proudly. "He's got nerves of steel. See you at the race!"

SpongeBob realized the competition was getting fierce.

SpongeBob blew his whistle. "Let's start with some sprints. On your mark, get set, go!"

Gary barely moved.

"Come on, Gary!" shouted SpongeBob. "You've gotta start training if you're going to win." Just then Squidward peeked in.

"Don't waste your breath, SpongeBob. That mongrel of yours doesn't have a chance," Squidward said confidently.

"All right, Gary, no more fooling around," instructed SpongeBob. "Come on, move it! Up, up, up! Down, down, down! Faster, faster, faster! Go, go, go!"

The day of the race finally arrived.

"Well, SpongeBob, I didn't think your mongrel mutt would even find the starting line," snickered Squidward. "Congratulations."

"Save it for the loser's circle," said SpongeBob. "Gary happens to be in the best shape of his life."

Gary coughed and wheezed.

SpongeBob gave Gary his final pep talk. "Listen up. You're the undersnail. Everybody's already counting you out. Now, get out there and win!"

"Meow," muttered Gary.

"On your mark!" shouted the referee. "Get set! Slither!"

"And they're off," said the announcer. "Number six, Snellie, rockets out of the starting box, leaving the other two competitors in the dust."

"Go, Snellie! You got it, baby!" cheered Squidward.

SpongeBob was not having the same luck. Gary hadn't budged from the starting gate.

"What are you doing, Gary?" shouted SpongeBob. "The race has started. Let's go! Start moving! You're blowing everything we trained for!"

Patrick's snail was also at the starting line. "It's okay, Rocky," Patrick said. "You go when you feel like it."

Gary slowly began to move. He panted heavily as he trudged ahead. "Not good enough!" shouted his coach. "Faster!"

The more SpongeBob yelled, the faster Gary tried to go. But it was no use. Gary was exhausted.

"That coach is pushing that snail too hard," said the announcer.

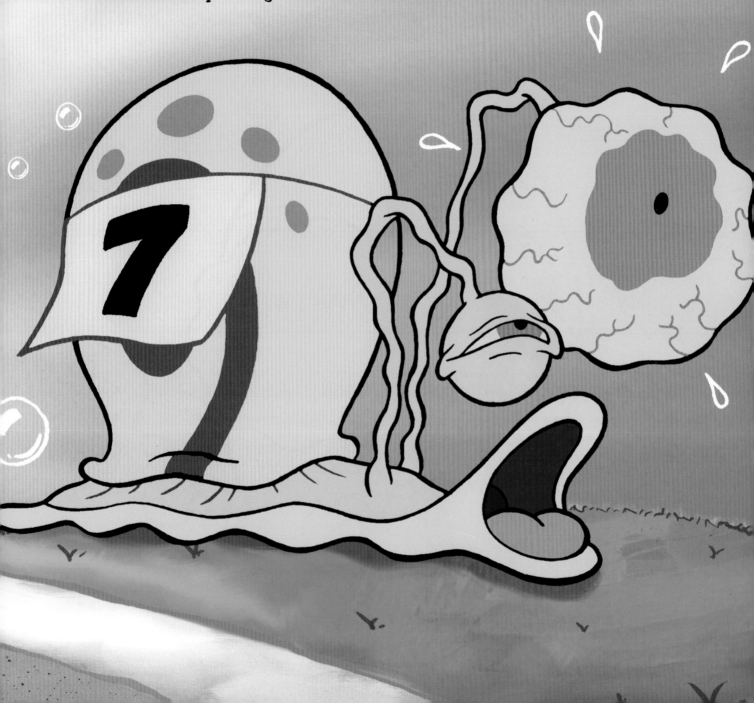

Suddenly, Gary's bloodshot eye popped like a tire!
"It looks like number seven has a blowout," said the announcer.
Shortly after, Gary's other eye blew.

"Make that two, folks," said the announcer.

"Uh . . . Gary, you can stop now," said SpongeBob.

Gary began to spin out of control — and headed straight for the wall! BAM!
The crowd gasped.

"Nooooooo!" shouted SpongeBob. "Hold on, Gary, I'm coming!"

SpongeBob raced to Gary's side.

"One of the coaches has raced onto the track. That is an automatic disqualification. Looks like number six has this race all wrapped up, ladies and gentlemen," said the announcer.

Squidward cheered. "Come on, Snellie. It's all you!"

"Oh, Gary," cried SpongeBob. "Why didn't you just say I was pushing you too hard?"

"Meow," said Gary.

"You did?" asked SpongeBob. "Oh, Gary, why didn't you tell me I wasn't listening?"

"Meow," answered Gary.

"You did? Oh, Gary!" wailed SpongeBob.

Suddenly, Squidward's prize snail stopped racing. She turned to look at Gary and then rushed to his side. The two snails looked into each other's eyes and purred.

"My oh my, folks," said the announcer. "I've never seen anything quite like it. It seems Snellie, the leader, just went back to comfort Gary."

"Looks like you and me are in-laws. Eh, Squidward?" said SpongeBob.

The crowd cheered as the winner crossed the finish line.

"But that's impossible," said Squidward. "If Snellie didn't win, then who did?"

"And the winner is," shouted the announcer, "Rocky!"

The crowd went wild! Patrick started to laugh until he cried.

Squidward moaned. "My purebred, which cost me seventeen hundred dollars, lost to a rock."

Patrick rushed to Squidward's side. "Don't worry, Squidward. I know how much you wanted to win, so I had the trophy engraved to you."

Squidward took the trophy in his tentacles. "Gosh, Patrick, thanks!" He looked at the plaque and read it out loud. " 'The first-place snail racing cup presented to Squidward *Tortellini*.' "

Patrick and SpongeBob happily put their arms around their friend. "Will I ever win?" grumbled Squidward.

SQUIDWARD
TORTELLINI